For Jordan Landrum.

— N. G.

I dedicate the book to the students of Marlboro elementary and
Balmville Elementary for posing as characters for this project. May all
children be inspired by all acts of kindness.

— B. C.

Published in 2017 by Eerdmans Books for Young Readers,
an imprint of Wm. B. Eerdmans Publishing Co.
2140 Oak Industrial Dr. NE, Grand Rapids, Michigan 49505
www.eerdmans.com/youngreaders

Text © 2017 Nikki Grimes
Illustrations © 2017 Bryan Collier

Manufactured in Malaysia

23 22 21 20 19 18 17   1 2 3 4 5 6 7 8 9

ISBN 978-0-8028-5445-2

A catalog record of this book is available from the Library of Congress.

Scripture quotation taken from The Holy Bible, New International Version® NIV® Copyright © 1973, 1978,
1984, 2011 by Biblica, Inc.™ Used by permission. All rights reserved worldwide.

The illustrations were created using paint and collage.

The
Watcher

Written by

Nikki Grimes

Illustrated by

Bryan Collier

Eerdmans Books for Young Readers

Grand Rapids, Michigan

Psalm 121

¹ I lift up my eyes to the hills—
    where does my help come from?
² My help comes from the LORD,
    the Maker of heaven and earth.
³ He will not let your foot slip—
    he who watches over you
    will not slumber;
⁴ indeed, he who watches over Israel
    will neither slumber nor sleep.

⁵ The LORD watches over you—
    the LORD is your shade at your right hand;
⁶ the sun will not harm you by day,
    nor the moon by night.
⁷ The LORD will keep you from all harm—
    he will watch over your life;
⁸ the LORD will watch over
    your coming and going
    both now and forevermore.

JORDAN

Some days, even the ant towers over me, and **I**

cower in a forest of grass, waiting for the fear to **lift**

like fog, so I can be brave, rise **up**.

But the class bully growls my name, and I shiver in **my**

sneakers, feel the wet fill my **eyes**.

Then I remember how Mom told me **to**

roll my fear like a ball, toss it high in **the**

air where you can catch it, and fling it to the **hills**.

TANYA

Wish I was some other Who, living **where**
stutterers aren't treated like spit. **Does**
that place even exist? No. So I switch off **my**
hearing when Grandma says to ask you for **help**.
If you care, maybe you can tell me how **come**
kids tease me into meanness I can't run **from**.

JORDAN

I wake, a hail of hot words hitting **my**

bedroom wall, like bullets. "God, **help**,"

I pray, hoping the answer **comes**

quickly. My heart bleeds **from**

the sound of my neighbors' war next door. **The**

sun and I both shrivel, hiding behind the **Lord**.

TANYA

I call my first eyeglasses a miracle, **the**

way words finally take shape. Grandma says my **Maker**

knew I wasn't stupid, understood the real root **of**

my problem, and whispered it from **heaven**,

told my teacher, who told Grandma, **and**

now, English is clear as sunrise over **earth**.

JORDAN

My stingy landlord doesn't notice **he**

dropped his wallet. If it warms my pocket, who **will**

know? I cuddle up with this thought—**not**

that my Sunday school lessons would ever **let**

me forget how keenly **your**

eye sees what my hand holds, where my **foot**

steps. Better give the wallet back before I **slip**.

TANYA

"Welcome, Israel," says our teacher. **He**
tells this kid with a weird accent to take a seat, but **who**
is it makes room for this geek? Everyone **watches**
to see, wonders why it's me who waves him **over**.
My answer? A snarl that says, "Mess with me. I dare **you**."

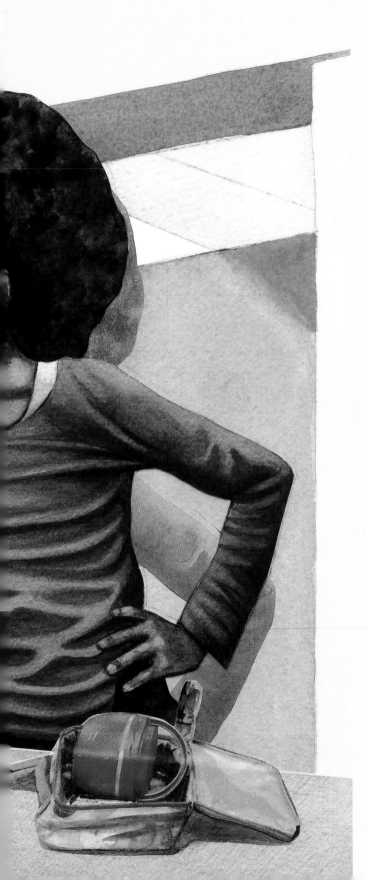

JORDAN

By noon, my belly's a balloon of fear. I figure Tanya **will** make this kid as miserable as me. I whisper in his ear, "Do **not** trust Tanya!" but she interrupts. "You two p-planning a s-**slumber** party? Fun!" I grit my teeth, but Israel smiles and says, "**Indeed**!"

TANYA

New kid hasn't heard anything bad about me. **He**

could maybe give me half a chance. That's all I want. **Who**

sees how I hurt without a friend? Who **watches**

when I fill my pillow with tears 'cause I'm so **over**

being lonely? Besides, the kid needs a protector, name like **Israel**.

JORDAN

Pain knocks in the night. Mom and Dad say my tonsils **will**

have to go, but I hate hospitals, and **neither**

can calm me, till Mom sings a silly lullaby about **slumber**.

I groan, then laugh, like always. "We won't leave you, **nor**

will God," she whispers, and I finally surrender to **sleep**.

TANYA

Grandma is sick, skin pale as cream, and she's **the**

only one who loves me. What if she— "The **Lord**

will hold your hand," she tells me. "He **watches**

out for all his children." She says it over and **over**,

pressing me to believe, whispers "God loves **you**."

JORDAN

Tanya always pricks like a splinter. Today, she snatches **the**

lunch with cookies Mom baked especially for me, but the **Lord**

must've told the principal, 'cause she shows up, asks "**Is**

there a problem here? If not, I believe **your**

class is about to begin." Empty-handed, Tanya runs for the **shade**

of the nearest tree, glares **at**

me when the principal isn't looking. "**Your**

luck's going t-t-to run out," she growls, then spits **right**

on the ground. I feel a fist forming. "Lord, take my **hand**."

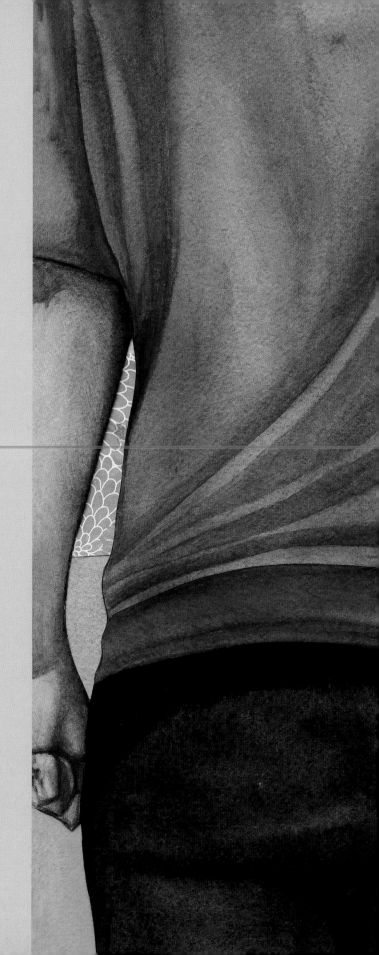

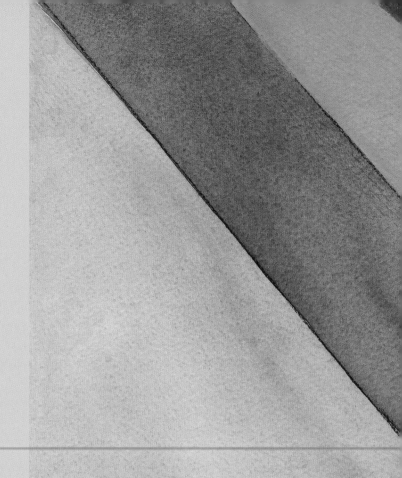

TANYA

My stupid stomach screams hungry, **the**

toast I had for breakfast forgotten by the time the **sun**

hits the middle of the sky. What **will**

I do for dinner while Grandma's sick? I know I'm **not**

supposed to steal or cause anybody **harm**,

but I'm starving and—What? Here comes Jordan. "**You**

want half a sandwich?" I don't answer, but he leaves it **by**

my book bag, hurries to his desk. Shame gnaws at me all **day**.

JORDAN

People are puzzles, even Tanya—not all good, **nor**

all bad, but mixed. I try not to care, but **the**

Lord pokes me with his Word, mentions the **moon**

Tanya and I both sleep under, dream **by**.

God loves us the same, tucks us both in at **night**.

TANYA

I flip my angry switch, push Jordan whenever **the**

kid comes close. But he won't scare now, just whispers, "**Lord**,

I hear you," then smiles. Sometimes he tells me, "I **will**

pray for you." Won't even laugh at my stutter! And why does he **keep**

bringing me cookies? One night, I ask Grandma, "Did **you**

tell his mom to make him be nice to me?" She looks up **from**

her Bible, beaming. "Maybe you should ask Jordan. **All**

I can tell you is that asking can't do any **harm**."

JORDAN

Israel boards the school bus, waves to me as **he**

passes by Tanya, who looks like she might cry. **Will**

she ever find a friend? My sudden worry a wonder, I **watch**

myself, like some stranger, rise and march right **over**

to sit beside my old enemy, because you tell me **your**

plan for her includes something nicer than a lonely **life**.

TANYA

Dizzy with questions, I'm afraid to speak. **The** only word I get out is "Why?" Jordan shrugs. "The **Lord** told me to. But if you really want me to leave, I **will**." "No. Stay," I whisper, my insides melting while I **watch** my new—friend?—ease into a smile and wave Israel **over**.

JORDAN

Tanya's attendance is perfect at dinnertime. "**Your**

mom's a good cook" is her excuse for **coming**

over every other day. But I don't mind, **and**

Mom's glad to see how strong this friendship is **going**.

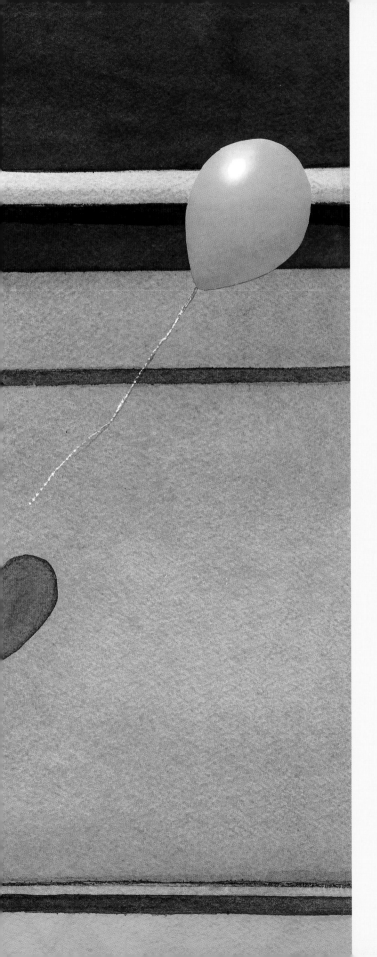

TANYA

Jordan and I stretch out in the forest of grass, **both** imagining adventures we could have in the clouds. **Now** that I'm still enough to notice, I feel the Lord here **and**— no lie—he whispers, "I'm with you now and **forevermore**."

Poetry Form

The Watcher is written in a form of poetry called the **golden shovel**. In this form, you take lines from an existing poem or, as in this book, from a psalm, and create a new poem using the words from the original. First, you choose the line you want to use, and then arrange the words, one by one, in the right margin like this.

in
the
beginning

Then, write new lines, with each line ending in one of these words. The words have to be in the same order as the original. In this example, that would mean the first line of the new poem would end in the word "in," the second line would end in the word "the," and the last one would end in the word "beginning."

Dawn breaks, and sunbeams tiptoe **in**
scattering bits of light across **the**
room, whispering "A new day is **beginning!**"

Notice how the new poem stands completely on its own, while using each of the original words chosen. If the line you choose has three words in it, you will end up with a three-line poem. If you choose a line with five words in it, you'll end up with a five-line poem, and so on.

This can be a tricky way to create a poem, but it can also be lots of fun. Give it a try!

— Nikki Grimes